POTLUCK

By Anne Shelby

Pictures by Irene Trivas

ISBN: 0-673-80541-7

Child-sized version of *Potluck* published in 1993 by
Scott, Foresman and Company.

Printed in the United States of America.
  2345678910-KPH-9998979695949392

**Scott, Foresman
and Company**

Editorial Offices:
Glenview, Illinois

Regional Offices:
Sunnyvale, California
Tucker, Georgia
Glenview, Illinois
Oakland, New Jersey
Carrollton, Texas

Alpha and Betty decided to
have a potluck. So—
they called up their friends,
cleaned up their house,

4

and set their table– for thirty-one.
Finally...

Acton appeared with
asparagus soup.

Ben brought bagels.

Cc

Christine came with carrot cake
and corn on the cob.

Don did dumplings.

Ee

Edmund entered
with enchiladas,

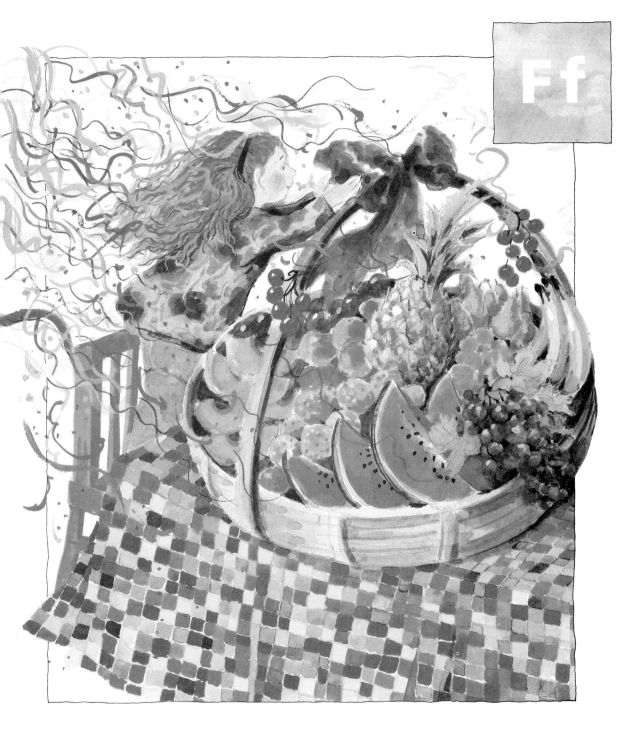

followed by Fran,
who furnished fruit.

Graham had gone by Garbanzo's
Bakery to get good garlic bread.

12

H.B. had made honey-sweetened hot tea. Irene insisted on iced.

June joined in with jelly rolls;

Kim with a kettle of kale.

15

Lonnie loves lasagna, so he brought lots of that.

Mm

Monica made mounds and
mounds of mashed potatoes.

Norman knew that oodles of noodles would be needed.

Oo

Otis offered onions;

Priscilla, a peanut-butter pie.

Qq

Quincy, of course,
brought quiche;

Rose, her famous rice
and raisin recipe.

Sam showed up with spaghetti sauce subtly seasoned with spices.

The triplets turned up with tacos;
Ursula, with upside-down cake.

Victor ventured vegetarian stew,
while Wally wowed the crowd
with his wonderful waffles.

Xx **Yy**

Xavier brought some excellent
examples of extra-special
X-shaped cookies. Yolanda said
yes to yams and yogurt.

But somebody was missing. Who?
Then, at the last minute...

Zeke and Zelda zoomed in with zucchini casserole.

So they all sat down and ate and
ate and ate and ate and ate and ate.

They ate everything from A to Z.